Chapter 1

The ball slammed into the back of the net. It was another goal to Saxton Rovers.

'Oh no!' said Gizmo. 'I can hardly bear to watch.'

Andy joined Gizmo at the touchline. 'What's the score now?' he asked.

'Don't ask,' said Gizmo, gloomily.

The referee blew his whistle. It was the end of the match. The players shook hands and ran off the pitch. A few people cheered the winning team off the field. Nobody cheered Wolf Hill Wanderers.

'Five nil!' sighed Gizmo. 'It's our worst defeat all season.'

Gizmo's dad managed Wolf Hill Wanderers. The club was having a hard time.

'We need new players,' said Mr
Harding. 'The club house roof is
leaking. We need new goal nets. We've
lost the team coach. We need
something to pep the club up.'

'We need to raise some money,' said
Gizmo.

'We certainly do,' agreed Mr
Harding. But how?'

'I know,' said Gizmo. 'Why don't we organize a celebrity football match?'

'What do you mean – a celebrity football match?' asked Andy.

'Well, you get famous people to form a team – pop stars, sportsmen and people like that,' replied Gizmo. 'Then they play Wolf Hill Wanderers. People pay to come and watch it.'

Mr Harding rubbed his chin. 'You know, that's a pretty good idea,' he said.

Chapter 2

A week later, Andy and his mum went past Mr Harding's shop. Gizmo and Mr Harding were standing outside.

Gizmo pointed at the shop front. 'It's all our own work. What do you think of it?' asked Gizmo, proudly.

In the window was a poster. In huge letters were the words, 'Celebrity Football Match, Saturday, 15th October, 2pm.'

Andy's mum stepped back and read out loud. 'Meet the stars.' She looked at Mr Harding and asked, 'So which stars have agreed to take part?'

Mr Harding coughed, 'Ah . . . well,' he said. 'There's the new Mayor, and then there's Paul Fox who runs the Motocross Park, his son Peter and . . . er . . . '

'Don't forget Mr Saffrey,' added Gizmo.

'But are there any *real* celebrities?' asked Andy.

'Well . . . er . . . not exactly,' began Mr Harding. 'But I've written lots of letters. I'm still waiting for the replies.'

'So, you've got nobody really famous?' said Andy's mum.

Mr Harding looked uncomfortable. 'Not yet,' he said.

'Well, you won't sell many tickets if you can't get some big names,' smiled Andy's mum.

'I know. I know,' said Mr Harding. 'But I've still got three weeks to go, so don't worry. I'm working on it.'

Chapter 3

The light hung in the sky over Wolf Hill Park. It was bigger and brighter than a star and it was a greenish yellow colour.

At first, Andy thought it was an aircraft. Then, as he watched it, he noticed something strange. It was not moving. It just seemed to stay in one spot as if it was hovering in the sky.

10

Andy went inside and called his mum. 'Come and see this odd-looking light in the sky,' he gasped.

Andy's mum came out and looked up into the sky. She watched the light for a few minutes. From time to time it moved a little as if it was swaying. Then its colour changed slightly.

'It's moving, but not very much,'
said Andy's mum. 'It's either
spinning, or it's going round and
round in a tight circle.'

Andy ran along to Gizmo's flat but
Gizmo wasn't in. 'He's gone out with
his dad,' said Mrs Harding.

Andy ran back to his flat. The light
in the sky was beginning to sway
from side to side. 'It's really weird,'
said Andy. 'I wonder what it can be.'

Jools came out with some binoculars. He focused them on the light. 'It seems to have a shape,' he said. 'It looks like an object of some sort.'

'Let me see,' said Andy, excitedly.

Jools gave him the binoculars.

Andy tried to focus them, but he had a job to adjust them. At that moment the light suddenly dipped.

Then it dropped out of sight.

'Oh! It's gone,' gasped Andy. 'I missed it.'

Jools looked excited. 'It was amazing,' he said. 'It was round and flat, like a dish. I think it was a UFO.'

Chapter 4

The next day, Andy told Kat and Arjo about the light. 'It just seemed to hang in the sky,' he said. 'Jools said it looked like a UFO.'

'I wish I'd seen it,' said Arjo.

Loz was listening. 'Nan and I saw it, too,' she said. 'Nan thought it was a helicopter.'

'I suppose it could have been,' agreed Andy.

'What does UFO stand for?' asked Loz.

'It means Unidentified Flying Object,' replied Andy. 'I've got a book about them at home.'

'Are they the same as flying saucers?' asked Loz.

'I don't think so,' said Andy. 'A UFO can be anything in the sky – like a flock of birds – but no one can tell what it is. Flying saucers are supposed to be spacecraft.'

'That's right,' added Kat, 'they come from outer space – from Mars, or somewhere.'

'They have little green men in them,' joked Andy.

'I don't believe in flying saucers,' said Kat. 'Why don't they ever land? Why fly all the way from outer space, then not make contact with us?'

Andy pretended to be an alien. He held two pens on the top of his head. They looked like stalks. 'Greetings, Earthlings!' he said in a squeaky voice. 'Take me to your leader.'

Everyone laughed.

Chapter 5

Two days later, the light in the sky was back. Once again it appeared over Wolf Hill Park. This time it was Arjo who saw it. He ran into the house.

'It's that UFO again,' he said excitedly.

Kat and Arjo ran outside. Their dad
joined them. They all stared at the
light. It stayed in the same place. It
looked as if it was hovering over the
park. Every so often it seemed to
swing from side to side.

'Do you think it's a flying saucer?'
asked Kat.

Mr Wilson laughed. 'I shouldn't think so,' he said.

The light moved. It went slowly sideways. Then it suddenly dipped down out of sight.

'I wonder if it's landed somewhere,' said Arjo.

Arjo was excited. He pulled his dad's sleeve. 'Let's go up to Wolf Hill Park,' he said. 'Maybe we could see it.'

Mr Wilson shook his head. 'It's much too dark,' he said. 'Besides, it's probably a helicopter. It will have gone by now.'

All over Wolf Hill, people were talking about the UFO. Dozens of people had seen it. A reporter from the local newspaper talked to some of them.

'It looked like a flying saucer,' one man said. 'It just hung in the sky as if it was looking down at something. Then it dipped down as if it was landing.'

Chapter 6

Andy saw it first. He gave a gasp and ran towards the middle of the football pitch. 'Come and look at this,' he yelled. He began to point and wave his arms.

He was pointing at some strange marks. They were plain to see, even at distance.

Gizmo ran on to the pitch, too.

'How weird!' he exclaimed. 'What on earth are they?'

In the grass, were six round yellowish marks about the size of dustbin lids. They formed a large circle. In the centre of the circle, the grass was blackened and scorched as if it had been burned.

Other people ran up to look at the peculiar marks in the grass.

Mr Harding scratched his head. He bent down to examine the pitch. 'It looks as if something's killed the grass,' he said. 'But what?'

Jason, the team captain, looked uneasy. 'People saw something strange in the sky over here,' he said. 'It can't be. You don't think . . .' He blinked and shook his head.

'Think what?' asked Mr Harding.

'That a UFO landed on the pitch,' said Jason.

.   .   .   .

News of the strange marks spread like wildfire.

Mr Wilson took Kat and Arjo to see them. They found that dozens of people had got there before them.

Mr Harding was making sure
people didn't get too close to the
marks. He had put a large circle of
rope on stakes round them.

Gizmo and Andy ran over. Andy's face was red with excitement. He pointed to the pitch. 'I saw the marks first,' he said.

Kat pointed to the round patches in the grass. 'Could they have been made by the UFO's landing feet?' she asked.

'They must have been,' said Andy.

'What do you think burned the grass?' asked Arjo.

'Maybe the UFO has some kind of motor that gives out heat,' said Gizmo.

A photographer from the local newspaper arrived. He took a picture of the marks.

A reporter spoke to Mr Harding. 'Do you think a UFO could have landed here?'

Mr Harding shrugged. 'Who knows!' he said. 'But I'll tell you what.' He paused for a second. 'I'm going up on top of Wolf Hill tonight. If the UFO comes back it will be a good place to watch it.'

Chapter 7

That evening, Arjo and Kat begged their dad to take them to Wolf Hill.

'Please let's go UFO spotting,' Dad,' urged Arjo. 'Think what it would be like to see one.'

In the end, Mr Wilson agreed.

Kat and Arjo put on warm sweaters. Mr Wilson found a torch and a pair of binoculars and they set out in the car.

They had hoped to drive to the top of Wolf Hill. But they couldn't. The gate across the track that led to the top was locked.

Cars were parked at the bottom of the hill. People were climbing over the gate and walking up. Mr Wilson got out of the car.

'We'll just have to walk up, too,' he said. 'Bring the torch and that rug.'

'We are not the only ones to come UFO spotting,' said Kat. 'Everybody else has had the same idea.'

It was a moonlit night, but it was quite windy. Sometimes the moon went behind clouds that scudded across the sky.

There were about four hundred people sitting or standing all over the top of the hill. Most of them had binoculars. More people were walking up the track.

At the top of the hill they met Andy. He was with Jools. They found a spot and all sat together. From the hill they looked down on the football pitch.

There was a low buzz of conversation. Everybody spoke in hushed voices. It was as if they were afraid that any noise would keep the UFO away.

Time passed slowly. Arjo, Kat and Andy began to get restless and fidgety.

'How long will we have to wait?' whispered Arjo.

'Maybe forever,' laughed Mr
Wilson. 'UFOs probably don't exist.'

'I need to go behind a bush,' said
Arjo.

'So do I,' said Andy.

Mr Wilson picked up the torch. 'I'll
come, as well,' he said.

Jools stood up. 'And me,' he said.

The four of them walked across to
a small copse. The moon went
behind the clouds and it grew
suddenly darker.

Mr Wilson shone the torch in front
of them. They all stopped. There was
a sound in the bushes ahead.

Something was moving in the
darkness. It was something strange
and frightening . . .

Chapter 8

Mr Wilson shone the torch in a slow arc. The beam of light stopped. Standing behind some bushes was a figure. Everyone froze. Arjo grabbed his dad's hand. Andy felt his skin go cold.

The figure was not human. It was a
creature of some sort – an alien. It
was quite small, with a greenish
brown body covered in scales. At the
top of a long, thick neck it had a
large flat head. Its huge eyes glinted
in the torchlight.

Mr Wilson stepped back with a
gasp. His foot sank in a hole and he
fell heavily. The torch flew out of his
hand. It went out as it hit the ground.

Arjo grabbed the torch and it came on, but the light was dim. Arjo shone the torch towards the bushes. But the creature had gone.

They all ran back to Kat. Andy's heart was pounding. Arjo was waving his arms.

'What on earth's the matter?' asked Kat.

'We've seen a space creature,' Arjo said. His voice squeaked as he spoke.

'It's true,' panted Andy. 'It was an alien, with a long neck and huge eyes.'

Kat grinned. 'Nice one, but pull the other leg,' she said. 'I wasn't born yesterday.'

'It's true, Kat,' said Mr Wilson. 'We all saw it. It was looking at us out of the darkness.'

'You planned this little joke,' laughed Kat.

'No, honestly,' said Jools. 'It's no joke. It was an alien all right.'

Suddenly there was shouting further up the hill. Some people were talking and yelling excitedly. 'I saw something through the night binoculars,' shouted one. 'It was a creature of some sort.'

'I saw it, too,' yelled another. 'It was like an alien.'

'We all saw it,' called someone else. 'It was running down the hill.'

Jools ran to the people. 'Was it a smallish creature, like a space alien?' he asked. 'We saw it, too. It was in the copse behind us.'

A buzz of excited talking spread from group to group. 'Who has a

torch?' yelled a man. 'Let's go after it.
See if we can find it.'

'Is that a good idea?' said a voice.
'Is it safe? What if it's not friendly?
What if it's armed?'

'It may be radioactive, or
something,' said another voice.

Some of the excitement vanished. A few people felt concerned and a little afraid. The uneasy feeling spread to Jools and Mr Wilson.

Jools picked up the rug. 'I think we'd better go,' he said. 'I don't want to expose Andy to anything nasty or dangerous.'

'We ought to tell the police or someone about this,' said Mr Wilson. 'If there is an alien out there, something should be done.'

'Will they believe you?' asked Kat. 'I didn't.'

'Enough people saw the creature,' replied Jools. 'They'll have to believe us.'

Chapter 9

The next morning Kat and Arjo met Loz. The alien was the only topic of conversation. 'It was really close to us,' said Arjo.

'I wish I'd seen it,' said Loz. 'Tell me again what it looked like.'

They saw Andy coming up Wolf Street. 'Have you seen Gizmo?' he asked. 'He wasn't at home. I wanted to ask him if he knew about the alien.'

'Let's go to the den,' suggested Loz. 'Andy can draw a picture of it, and Arjo can help.'

'Good idea,' said Andy.

The den was an old air raid shelter. Loz's great-grandmother let them use it. When they got there, they noticed something odd. The flat wooden cover over the steps was open.

'Funny,' exclaimed Loz. 'Someone's down there. I wonder who?'

They looked down into the den. A figure moved out of the shadows. Loz gave a cry. Andy gasped and sprang back. 'Oh no!' breathed Kat.

At the bottom of the steps was the alien. Its huge eyes seemed to be staring up at them. Arjo's voice went high with fright. 'It's the creature, again,' he squeaked.

The alien raised its arm as if in greeting and began to move up the steps. They all backed away, staring at it. Suddenly Andy pointed down.

'It's got human feet!' he exclaimed. 'I'd recognize those socks anywhere.'

'Greetings, Earthlings!' said a voice from inside the alien.

'I'd recognize that voice, too,' yelled Kat. 'It's Gizmo!'

'Gizmo!' shouted Andy. 'What are you doing dressed up as an alien?'

Chapter 10

Gizmo had taken off the alien's costume. He sat in his shorts and tee shirt facing the others.

'I almost died when you came up those steps,' said Loz. 'You looked so real.'

Arjo felt the arm of the alien suit. 'It looks brilliant,' he said. 'What's it made of?'

'It's made of latex. It does up at the back with velcro,' said Gizmo. 'I can see out from a panel in the neck. The alien's face rests on top of my head.'

'It's so realistic,' said Loz. 'The eyes are amazing.'

'My dad hired it from a film company. He wanted to wear it himself, but it was too small. It fitted me perfectly. It's pretty hot and stinky inside,' laughed Gizmo.

'But why? I don't get it,' said Andy. 'All this stuff about UFOs. Then the strange marks on the football pitch. What's going on?'

'It's for the football match today,' said Gizmo. 'Dad wanted publicity for it. Do you see? Hundreds of people will have seen the posters by now.'

'That's true!' said Kat. 'There was a giant poster at the football club. You could even see it from the top of the hill.'

'That was the idea,' said Gizmo. 'Think of all the people on the hill last night; and all the people who went to see the marks on the pitch.'

'But how did those strange marks get there?' asked Loz.

'Dad used bleach to kill the grass. He scorched the rest with a blow torch,' grinned Gizmo. 'Clever, eh?'

'So, how did he make that light in the sky?' asked Arjo.

'He didn't make it,' said Gizmo. 'We think it was a helicopter. But when everyone thought it might be a UFO he had the idea.'

'What about the alien costume?' asked Kat.

'We thought people would see it as a huge practical joke,' said Gizmo. 'Anyone can see it's just a latex suit. I was even wearing trainers so I could run fast. We didn't think people would take it seriously.'

Kat began to laugh. 'Arjo and Andy did,' she said. 'You should have seen their faces when they came out of those bushes last night.'

'So what happens now?' asked Andy.

Gizmo made them promise to keep all this a secret. He told them he was going to appear at the match in his alien costume. 'Dad's hoping loads of people will turn up later today,' he said.'

'Be careful,' warned Kat. 'People were pretty scared last night. I just hope you and your dad know what you are doing.'

Chapter 11

Mr Harding and Gizmo were in the Wolf Hill Wanderer's clubhouse. Gizmo struggled into the alien's costume. 'I hope this is the last time,' grumbled Gizmo. 'It pongs inside this suit.'

Mr Harding looked at Gizmo. 'Put on the rubber feet,' he ordered.

'Oh Dad, do I have to? Can't I wear trainers?' moaned Gizmo. 'It's hard to run in those flappy rubber feet. They're like flippers.'

Mr Harding put his hand on the alien's shoulder. 'This is the big one, son,' he said proudly. 'There are masses of people out there and we need the publicity. Just remember, you're doing this for the good of Wolf Hill Wanderers.'

The alien's head had slipped. A muffled voice came out of its neck. 'Mmmns . . . mmmns,' it said.

Mr Harding went to the door. 'I'm off,' he said. 'Wait for ten minutes before you run out. Make sure everyone sees you. Then slip through the gap in the hedge. I'll be waiting for you in the car.'

'Mmmns . . . mmmns,' said the alien.

.   .   .   .

Kat, Loz, Andy and Arjo looked down from the top of Wolf Hill. Andy had persuaded Jools to take them up there. They had let Jools into the secret.

Jools had laughed when they told him. 'You've got to hand it to Gizmo's dad,' he said. 'He's pulled off a good stunt. I wish him luck.'

Andy looked down at the club through the binoculars. He watched Mr Harding come out of the clubhouse. 'Gizmo should appear soon,' said Andy. 'There are loads of people watching.'

At that moment a fleet of army lorries and trucks roared into the football ground. Dozens of soldiers jumped down. They began to form a cordon round the pitch.

Four people got out of a car. They had on all-over white suits and wore breathing masks. They walked towards the middle of the pitch. One of them held a geiger counter.

A man's voice boomed through a loud hailer. 'This is the Ministry of Defence. Clear the area! Clear the area! You may all be in danger. The football ground is declared out of bounds! Clear the area now!'

The scientists in white suits began to put a plastic tent up over the marks.

'This looks serious,' exclaimed Jools. 'The publicity stunt has backfired. I bet Alan Harding didn't reckon on this happening.'

. . . .

In the club house, Gizmo was scared. He saw the soldiers through the window and heard a voice saying

'Clear the area.'

He tried to get out of the alien suit, but he couldn't. It was hard to do it with the creature's hands on. The fingers were bendy and long, and the hands firmly fixed on with velcro.

He decided to make a run for the hedge, just like his dad had told him. He pushed open the club house door and began to run.

People were filing away from the football ground. They were talking in hushed voices. Some of them looked worried.

Suddenly a shout went up. 'There it is. It's the creature!' Everyone watched as the alien ran across the back of the football pitch.

It ran in a funny way, picking up its feet as if the ground was red hot.

A marksman picked up a tranquillizer gun. He aimed it at the creature.

From the hill, Kat screamed. 'It's Gizmo! Don't shoot!'

The marksman fired.

Gizmo felt a pain in his bottom, as if he had been stabbed by a hot needle. He ran towards the hedge. He felt as if he was floating up into the air, high, high above Wolf Hill. Then nothing – just sleep.

Chapter 12

Gizmo laughed as he looked at all the newspapers. In some, the story was on the front page. There were photographs of him. His favourite story was:

Wolf Hill G

U FOoled

There were red faces at the Ministry of Defence today after hoax reports of a UFO landing at Wolf Hill were taken seriously. Soldiers and government scientists rushed to a football club only to find that an eleven year old boy, Matthew Harding and his father had staged an elaborate publicity stunt.

Andy, Loz and Kat called at the flat. Mr Harding let them in.

'You've seen the papers, then,' said Andy. 'You're famous, Gizmo.'

Loz looked concerned. 'My heart stopped when they shot a tranquillizer dart at you. Are you all right, now?' she asked.

'I'm fine,' said Gizmo. 'Only the tip of the dart went in. The thick rubber of the suit saved me. I was only out for about ten minutes.'

'Thank goodness!' said Kat.

Gizmo grinned. 'It turned out all right in the end,' he said. 'Dad's had a phone call from one of the newspapers. They want to sponsor a really big celebrity football match next month. They say it will make a good follow-up story.'

'So will they get some proper famous people?' asked Kat.

'I'm sure they will,' said Gizmo. 'And I bet loads of fans will come to watch.'

'Now you're famous, can you arrange for us to meet some of the celebrities?' asked Andy.

Conclusion

The celebrity football match was a huge success. An enormous crowd turned up to watch.

'I can't believe I'm so close to so many famous people,' gasped Loz.

At half time, Gizmo ran on to the pitch in his alien suit. Everybody cheered and clapped him. 'Good old Gizmo!' yelled Arjo.

None of the players took the match very seriously. The final score was two all.

A huge cheer went up. The players filed into the club house.

Gizmo's face was still red with excitement. He pushed his glasses back up his nose and made a 'thumb's up' sign at his dad.

Mr Harding looked at him, proudly.
'Well done, son,' he said. 'You were
brilliant as that alien. That's what
gave us the publicity. The whole
thing was a great success.'

Gizmo grinned at Andy. 'Fancy all
those people believing in aliens.'

'I don't know,' said Andy.
'Remember those lights in the sky?
We never did find out what they
really were.'

After the match, Andy and Gizmo helped Mr Harding take down the goal nets.

'It's getting dark,' said Mr Harding. 'Let's go.'

They locked up the clubhouse and made their way home.

A light hung in the sky over Wolf Hill Park. It was bigger and brighter than a star and it was a greenish yellow in colour.

The light didn't move. It just seemed to stay in one spot as if it was hovering in the sky.

Andy stared at it. 'It must be that helicopter,' he exclaimed.

'That's funny,' said Mr Harding. 'It doesn't look or sound like a helicopter.'

Level 1

The Hole in the Ground
Hidden Gold
The Flying Armchair
I Hate Computers!
The Night it Rained Chips
Toxic Waste

Level 2

Funny Sort of Treasure
Arjo's Bike
In the Net
Million-Dollar Egg
The Exploding Parrot
The Pool Party

Level 3

Siren Green
Remote Control
Blazing Burgers
Skydive Wedding
Electric Sandwiches
Copper Cockerel

Level 4

Who's Kooza?
Ghost
In the End
Let's Hear It for Nan
Hostage!
Dirt Bike Rider

Level 5

Black Holme Island
Who Kidnapped the Mayor?
Scottish Adventure
Alien
Sleepover Shock
Last Term at Wolf Hill